I0712778

Zoey and Clark's Adventures

To The British Virgin Islands

Written by: EJ Clark-Sledge

ALSO BY EJ CLARK-SLEDGE

Zoey and Clark's Adventures
To The North Pole

Zoey and Clark's Adventures
To Ireland

To my nieces Brooke and Laine and my nephew Adam. This book is dedicated to you with love. May its pages be a source of joy and countless adventures. I am grateful for your presence in my life and hope this story brings a touch of magic and laughter.

eBook: 979-8-9886861-6-3
Paperback: 979-8-9886861-7-0
Hardcover: 979-8-9886861-8-7

Library of Congress Control Number: 2023922642

Search and Find

"Wow! It's so beautiful here!" Zoey told Clark as the blue door quietly clicked shut behind her. Clark nodded. "It is, but . . . where is here?"

Looking around, Zoey's eye fell on a sign. "Welcome to the British Virgin Islands," Clark read. "Cool! The door brought us to an island!"
Welcome to the
British Virgin Islands

"Let's explore!" Zoey cried.

Soon, the cousins were splashing about in the water. "Check out these tunnels!" Clark said, and ducked to walk through one. "I don't think these are tunnels," Zoey said. "They look like giant boulders stacked on top of each other. I wonder where they came from."

"They're what remain of a mighty fight with the Kraken, many years ago." a melodious voice replied. Zoey and Clark spun around and found themselves face to face with the strangest creature they'd ever seen.

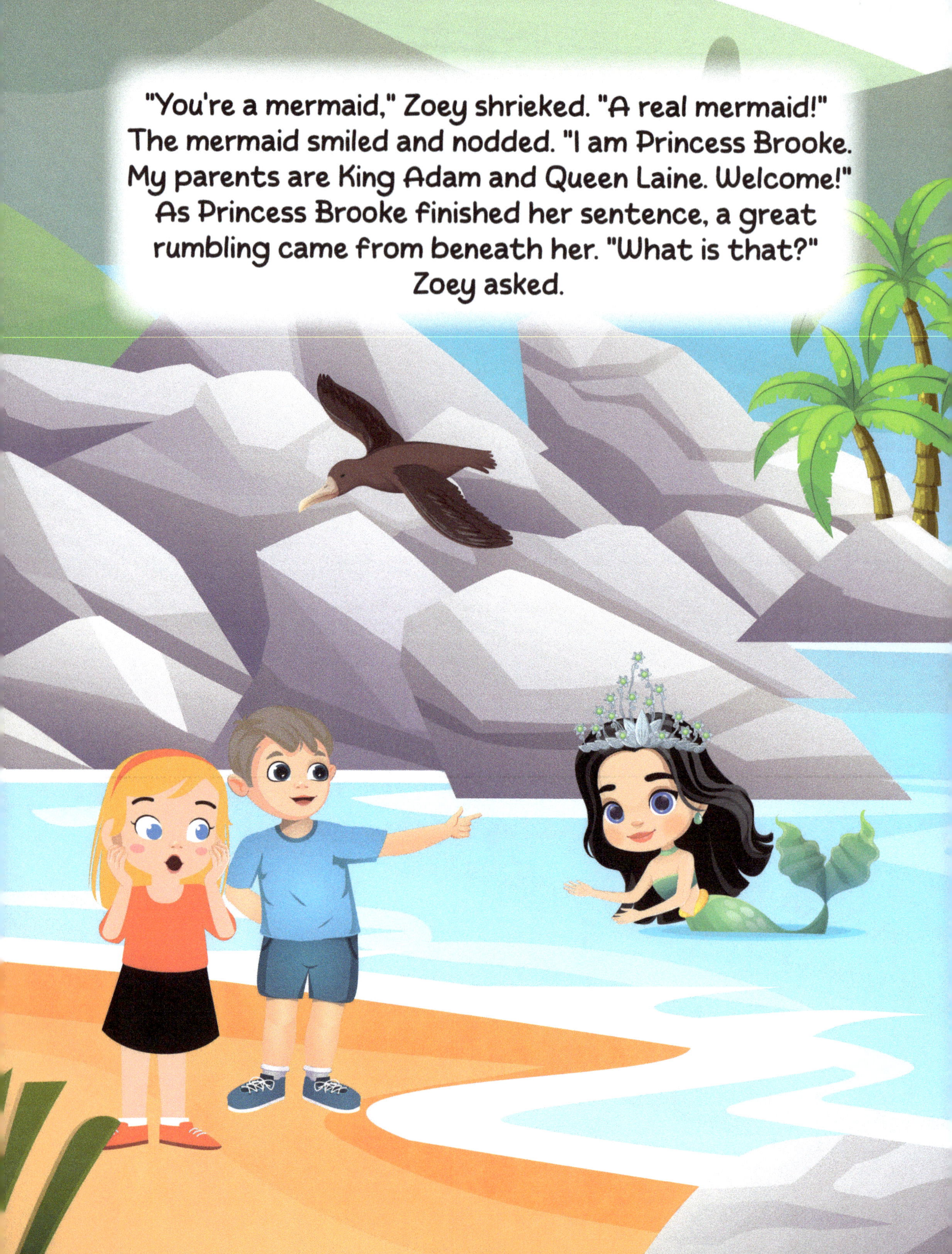

"You're a mermaid," Zoey shrieked. "A real mermaid!" The mermaid smiled and nodded. "I am Princess Brooke. My parents are King Adam and Queen Laine. Welcome!" As Princess Brooke finished her sentence, a great rumbling came from beneath her. "What is that?" Zoey asked.

Suddenly, a giant sea monster emerged from the water, giant boulders held in each of its 6 tentacles. "The Kraken!" Princess Brooke cried, her eyes as wide as starfish. "Quick! Take cover!"

Zoey and Clark sprinted behind the nearest boulders. They could only hope that the Kraken wouldn't think to look there. "Princess Brooke, where are you?" Zoey cried out. No response. "Did she leave us?" Clark asked, his voice trembling as much as the sand beneath them.

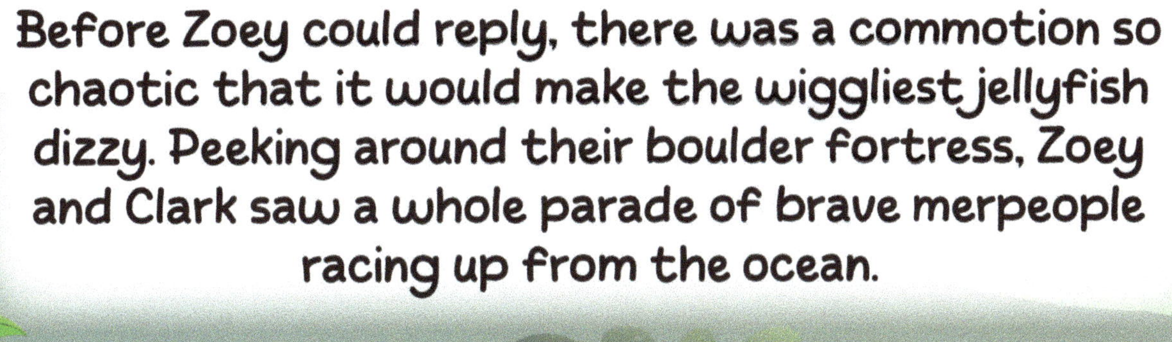

Before Zoey could reply, there was a commotion so chaotic that it would make the wiggliest jellyfish dizzy. Peeking around their boulder fortress, Zoey and Clark saw a whole parade of brave merpeople racing up from the ocean.

The merpeople leaped and twirled, making noises that sounded like squids on saxophones. "Look!" Zoey said, nudging Clark. "They're distracting the Kraken." Zoey was right. The Kraken couldn't take its eyes off the merpeople.

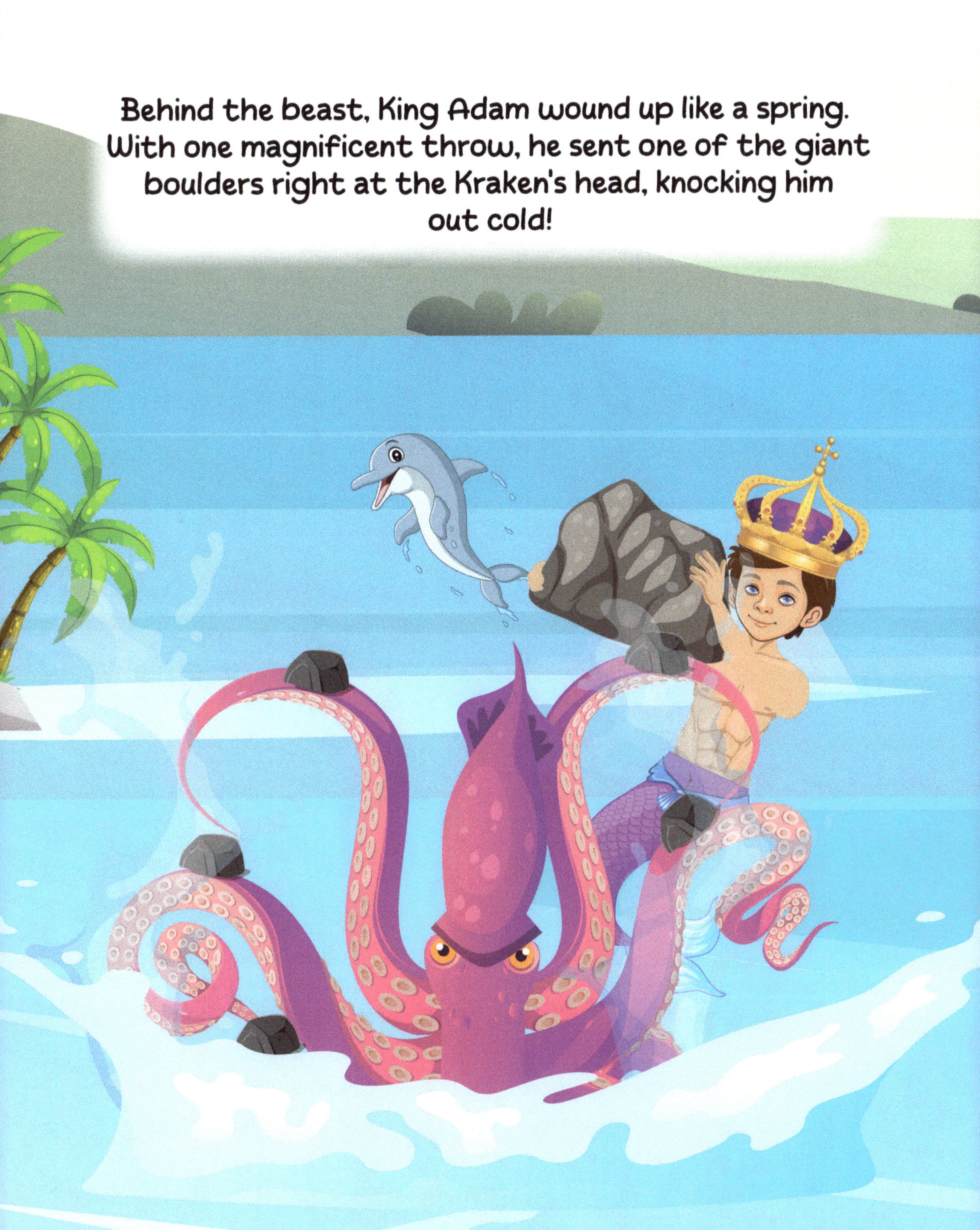

Behind the beast, King Adam wound up like a spring.
With one magnificent throw, he sent one of the giant
boulders right at the Kraken's head, knocking him
out cold!

"Quick!" Princess Brooke cried. "We need to seal him in a cave while he's still taking a Kraken-sized nap!" Princess Brooke took Zoey and Clark by the hand and dove into the water. To their surprise, they could breathe underwater as easily as they could breathe air.

The sensation of being underwater filled Zoey and Clark with a deep sense of peace and belonging. It was as if they were a part of the ocean, and it was more beautiful than anything they could have imagined.

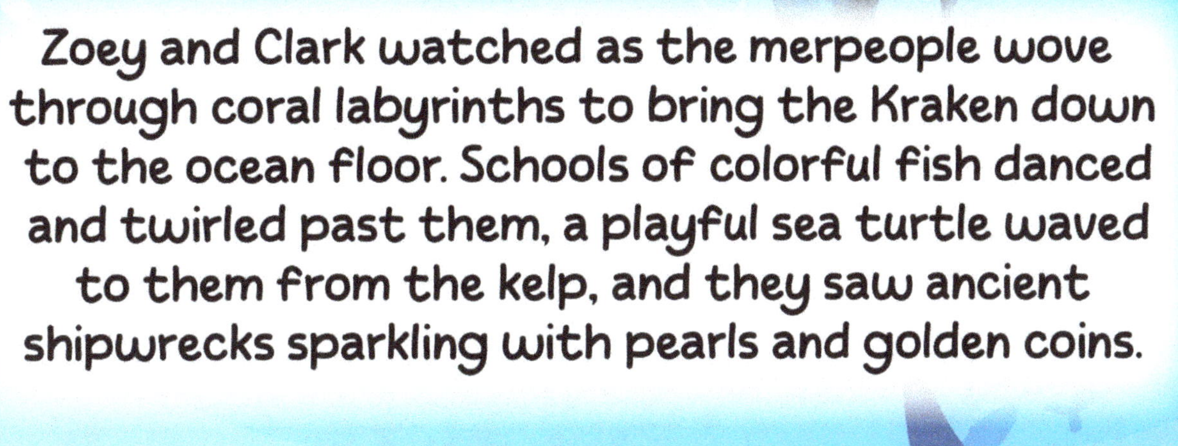

Zoey and Clark watched as the merpeople wove through coral labyrinths to bring the Kraken down to the ocean floor. Schools of colorful fish danced and twirled past them, a playful sea turtle waved to them from the kelp, and they saw ancient shipwrecks sparkling with pearls and golden coins.

At last, the King and
Queen pushed the
slumbering Kraken
into a large sea cave.

Swimming forward, Clark helped them push a colossal boulder in front of the cave entryway to seal the Kraken in. But before they could get the boulder in place, the monster began to wake.

The shaking cave walls threatened to come crashing down and Clark found himself too close to the side of the mountain. At that moment, a massive boulder began to tumble toward him.

Zoey watched in horror. If someone didn't do something
-and fast!-Clark would be crushed. "I've got him!"
Princess Brooke cried out. She swam faster than the
swiftest current, her hand grabbing Clark's just as
the boulder slammed into the ocean floor.

A cloud of sand and bubbles flew
into the water. When it cleared,
Zoey saw Princess Brooke and
Clark swimming safely away
from the cave.

With a wave of his trident, the King
sealed the Kraken inside the cave.
Around him, the merpeople erupted
in a joyful celebration. The Kraken
crisis was averted.

Princess Brooke returned Zoey and Clark back to the beach. "Thank you for your help," she said. "I am going to miss you two."

"We'll miss you, too! But at least we know you are all safe now," Zoey said. She hugged Princess Brooke, and watched as the mermaid dove back beneath the waves.

"Wow! That was amazing!" Zoey said when Princess Brooke was gone.
The Baths - Virgin Gorda

Suddenly there was a large POP and
the blue door reappeared on the sand.

"It sure was," Clark said. "And now it must be time for our next great adventure!" Zoey nodded and stepped toward the blue door. "I can't wait to see where it takes us next!"

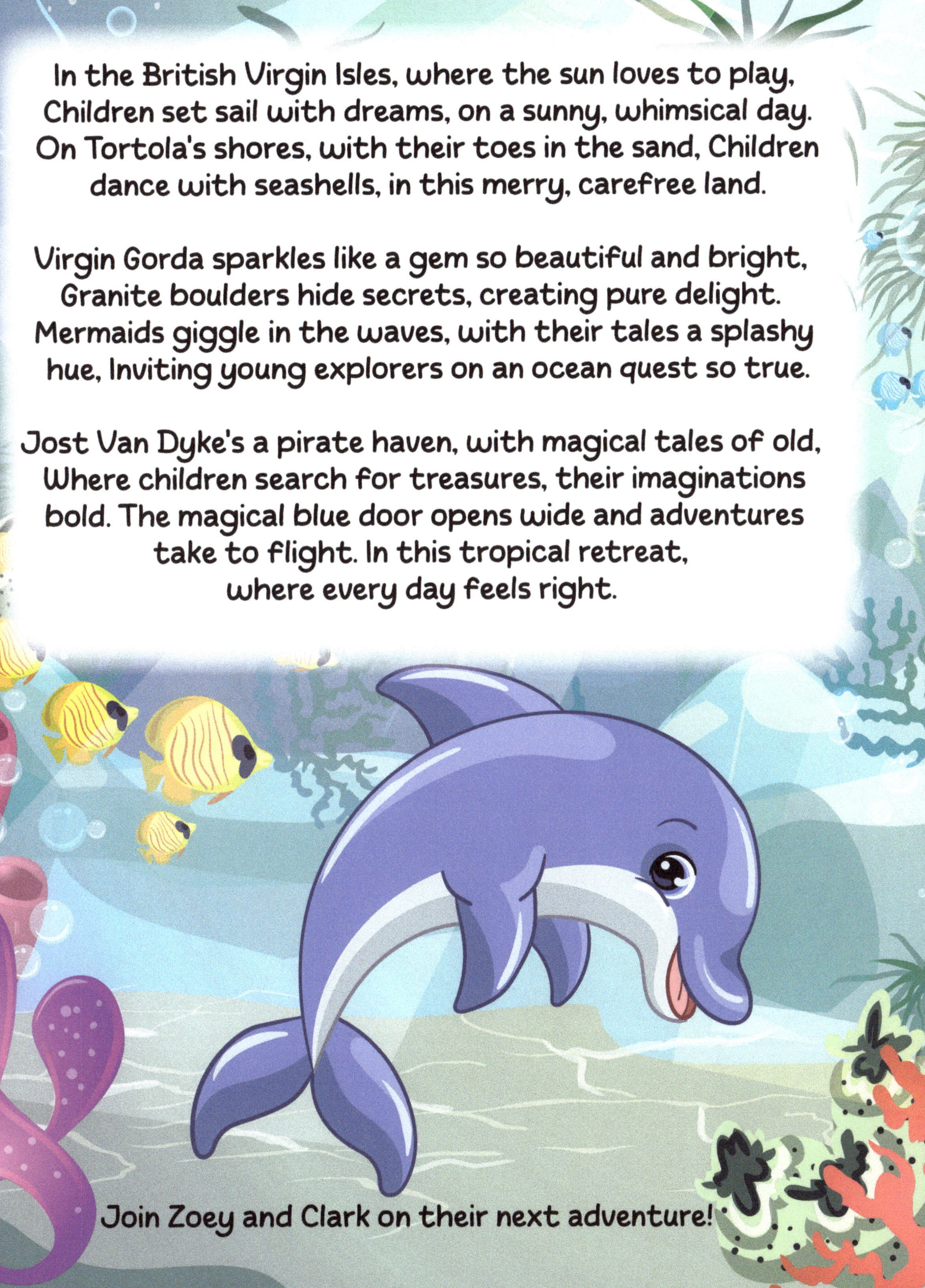

In the British Virgin Isles, where the sun loves to play,
Children set sail with dreams, on a sunny, whimsical day.
On Tortola's shores, with their toes in the sand, Children
dance with seashells, in this merry, carefree land.

Virgin Gorda sparkles like a gem so beautiful and bright,
Granite boulders hide secrets, creating pure delight.
Mermaids giggle in the waves, with their tales a splashy
hue, Inviting young explorers on an ocean quest so true.

Jost Van Dyke's a pirate haven, with magical tales of old,
Where children search for treasures, their imaginations
bold. The magical blue door opens wide and adventures
take to flight. In this tropical retreat,
where every day feels right.